MORNINGSTAR

Book Two~The Forbidden Bibles

MORNINGSTAR

Book Two~The Forbidden Bibles

ONDI LAURE

Disclaimer: Morningstar is a work of historical fiction. All names and characters are either invented or used fictitious. Any resemblance to actual persons is coincidental. To the best of the author's experience (her brush with death and her visit to an alternate dimension), heaven and our earthly realm are close. Moreover, while many events described in this book are historically accurate, God's boundless totality of being feminine, Sophia as much as being masculine, Jesus has yet to be authentically represented in historical scripture.

I dedicate this book to my daughters.

"I saw the Lord in a Vision and I said to him, Lord I saw you today in a vision. He answered and said to me. 'Blessed are you that you did not waver at the sight of Me. For where the mind is there is the treasure'."

The Gospel of Mary 5:8-9

Table of Contents

BOOK TWO II

CHAPTER ONE

Waxing Winds

The minute council came from the north: Charles, his three fellow knights, thirty archers, and the Earl of Northumberland, Lord Percy, made up their camp regiment assigned to gain King Richard, an Irish alliance. Though only intending to accompany the regiment to the tournament at Windsor that was being held in the expedition's honor, Lord Percy rode upon a glistening stallion as black as abysmal waters and as energetic as the lightning at sea. The remaining party marched. And march rapidly, for Lord Percy's horse continually overcame them, then departed ahead to relieve the stallion's exhilaration.

The May winds waxed and waned as they penetrated the emerald English countryside in their first week's march south. Aside from the lone outburst as the entourage left Leicester, they had no conflicts or skirmishes. A solitary young man called, "A pox on you, worthless scum! Might God's Blood be upon all ye at know thy Crown!"

from the top of a building at King Richard's extravagant display of men and lords. Charles and his men pretended not to hear the lad, for his arrest would mean his death in these treacherous times of King Richard's struggle for support. However, Lord Percy returned to the regiment from scouting ahead and heard some of the man's words. He rode beside Charles and stated, "The public must be reminded that any outspoken discontent toward King Richard is justification for treason." Lord Percy then shook his head, shrugged his shoulders, and turned his steed toward Windsor without giving any order to make an arrest.

The fact that Percy allowed this to go unpunished heightened Charles's suspicions of his Lord's disloyalty to King Richard.

Charles could not disagree more with the harsh orders to preserve respect for the King, but he scuffed his boots, failing to fulfill his solemnly sworn vow to protect the King. He shook his hair in the salty air that crept in from the sea as if to lose such thoughts of Lord Percy's disloyalty. As the commanding officer, Lord Percy was required to seize the boy. He had neglected the law.

Evening came upon them. They found a campsite with vantage points in all directions and a spring with fresh water for the men. The archers erected waxed linen tents for Earl Percy, Charles, and the other knights, but most men would sleep out in the open as summer was ushering out the rains of spring.

As he approached the Earl, the long march had done nothing to ease Charles's weary mind. "Lord Percy, I would like to offer my opinion of the day's progress. If I may, my Lord?" Charles, gnawing his lower lip, looked the Earl in the eye. "The boy today, who spoke out denouncing our King. I would like to make amends for that, my Lord."

The old colleagues sat silently, listening to the pop and hiss of a growing flame. The quiet company did not come naturally to the two men as it once had over the many assignments the court had sent them on together. Times had changed since their trek to London on King Richard's and Queen Anne's coronation day when Lord Percy's horse bolted, leaving him to walk—and their long ride together upon Charles's steed. Those days when laughter was in the air.

A ruckus among the men erupted nearby, disrupting the stillness of their thoughts. When they finally spoke, the tensions of the camp encompassed them.

"Lord Percy. I feel your energy for this expedition lessens with each stride, comrade. Are ye to tell me what is looming upon our horizon?" Charles remained sitting, closer now to the warmth of the flame.

"Charles, my friend and comrade, my king's man." Lord Percy derided. "Why the unease upon your breast?" He would not look into Charles's eyes. Shuffling his crisp new boots upon the stone, he continued to tell of his intentions, only affirming Charles's looming dread.

"My old friend. How I do respect you and your decisions! I offer for you to return at once to apprehend the lad back at Leicester and return him at once to face the consequences for his unjust remarks. You then may return home to the north," the Lord offered, knowing the indictment of the offer.

"And not accompany this regiment to Ireland, lord?" Charles loathed the words and spat them into the flames.

"Precisely, Charles. I shall not follow the fleet beyond the Irish Sea," Percy wrung his hands as if to rid them of sweat. "This is my offer to you, my friend.

In…" Lord Percy corrected himself. "In exchange for your daughter's betrothal to my son, Sir Percy," he declared more than he asked.

"Then ye, Lord Henry Percy of Northumberland, can obtain the outspoken youth on yer own return travels," Charles mimicked the plea recognized of Percy's request, "For I am fulfilling my sworn duty as a knight of King Richard's Court." Charles rose to his feet before adding. "Is this not to be an expedition to gain an alliance with the Irish? Peaceful, no doubt? What scheme has been unraveling along this road to Windsor, my old friend?" Charles asked. "Not a brilliant time to discuss marriage acquisitions," he added.

With his honorable and prideful nature, Charles failed to recognize the precise brilliance of Lord Percy's scheme. Lord Percy leaped to his feet, knocking a bucket of water on the ground. "Why, Knight?" The Lord stepped closer, leaned in, and whispered, "Would you have the lad put to death for speaking nothing but the truth? He was correct in all his remarks, Sir Charles. The King is not leading this country into anything but an alliance with France." Lord Percy began pacing nearer the fire. "Fetch more wood for our dinner, men," he commanded the crowd gathering around the flame. Once the company departed, the Earl continued, "Charles, we have been friends our lives through. It was our fathers who enlisted us together to King Richard's council. Times are growing restless. Our kingdom cannot keep funding the King's patronage of France and his lavish affairs. Taxes were to be lifted, not vindicated. Men fear the loss of their property and livelihoods if they can't come up with the monies." Percy emitted rage from his lips toward his comrade, knowing Charles disagreed.

"The King is aware of these matters, Lord Percy. Please, we must consider the King is attempting to align his trust from Parliament and what he is attempting to recount." Charles crouched at the tiny flame to stoke it with fuel. "The Roman Church threatens to execute anyone found reading the Bible in anything but Latin. Does it not do this to keep control of thy people and their monies?" Charles struggled to hide his desire to keep Lollard support upon the throne.

"What are you telling me, Charles?"

Charles raised his head to meet the Earl's eyes, "The King has no control of his Parliament, no doubt, sir. He is frustrated. And can do nothing without the Church's vote."

"King Richard rules our kingdom with indolence," Lord Percy declared. "His consistent apathy has cost the Englishman and the Scots far too dearly."

Lord Percy sat again near the small flame's glow, knowing the outcome of King Richard's impending departure sealed the fate of this militia. He scoffed, "I gave you an offer to return to Northumberland."

Charles listened, yet he held his breath as if holding his tongue. Then, the words escaped him readily. "What are you telling me, Percy? Has Henry Bolingbroke returned once more? I fear you may be leading us into uncertainty." Charles remained standing.

"There may be a wave of revenge upon our King, Charles. To right the wrongs perpetrated against him in December and on into this year," Percy reasoned.

"This is the reasoning for our King's continued activities, Lord? To gain the lost morale and to avenge those who opposed him?" Charles asked but did not wait for Sir Percy to elaborate. "Support that King Richard so desperately seeks for his lavish entourage; that is why we travel this day, is it not?" Charles questioned. And yet again, he continued without waiting for a reply. "All of these men and council who band together this day for spring's sojourn across the Irish Sea recognize this is their king's mission for the journey, to gain the alliance of the Irish," Charles spoke the truth. "And with King Richard is where my pledge was given and where it shall remain, for with him is our only support for the Lollard Society."

Lord Percy did not need to speak to confirm Charles's proclamation. He stood with his arms folded across his chest, swallowed hard with nostrils flared, and strode away, taking his secrets to brood upon.

Few could be entrusted with the ancient secrets that the Church herself could not be entrusted. Charles's father would say, "For one man, one family's spirit across the ages had been selected, perhaps randomly, perhaps by natural law." However, it became more evident to Lord Percy that there would be only one, and he knew now who. He had given him the choice for his return. *Perhaps we could have had all the power and control beyond the King and soon the new King. Power together, far greater than the Holy Church herself,* Percy cackled as he strode away from the fire. *But not to be had by Sir Charles, for he must be the righteous attendant to King Richard and sail west, leaving his daughter and her grandmamma as the sole guardians of his family's secret book.* His smile returned. "*Nothing but these weak women stand in my path.*" Lord Percy was en route to Windsor to witness the farewell of King Richard's entourage's venture across the Irish Sea. Lord Percy, eager to return north, kept his attention focused on the celebrations soon at hand. *The sacred* knowledge would soon be his, and the soon-to-be crowned King Henry Bolingbroke, his indentured servant.

CHAPTER TWO

Man's Greed

The stone house where Saren and her Grand Mamma lived – stood strong as the women. Though the night left little room for dreaming, Saren often woke as the moon's glow crowded out the stars and seeped through the gaps in the stone of the house's wall and beneath the door.

Her father was gone now, and the loneliness that filled her heart left an ache that even sleep could not erase.

Saren tossed upon the brittle straw mattress, praying that the dawn of day would bring her father home.

Somewhere in her bleakest moment, when tears were still ripe upon her cheek, she shut her eyes.

The stars that lingered penetrated the dark heavens as the great moon finally relinquished its dominance.

Saren woke with a surge of adrenaline as the sorrow of the night left with the moon's plight, though it would undoubtedly return. She rushed to peek out from the stone home to witness the remaining morning stars twinkling down upon her. Feeling refreshed, she recalled the glimmers of promise that had visited her slumber. She had dreamt and, therefore, was victorious over sleep, and the dreams gave her strength that sleep alone never could. She was renewed.

Rejoicing in the calm that her unconscious mind granted her in these subtle moments. She recalled dreams of plights of flight and images of feathered wings carrying her higher and higher into the moonlit night.

Saren shut her eyes in hopes that her dreams would return. The imagery did not, though the feeling of soaring did. She began her day confidently, imagining her father's pipe tune coming from the beach and missing him warmly. Still, she was burdened with her duties at home and her new obligation to protect her father's sacred book.

Fuel for their fire was sparse. Hunting wood along the roadways had also become a torturous task, and one dared not venture out alone or deep into a grove of trees. Being robbed, beaten, or worse was nothing less than certain.

Nan and Saren walked together through the thicket, searching for wood to fuel their cooking fire.

Music filled every moment together, as it had since Saren was a small child.

Music had accompanied them from her beginning—grand mamma's beginning, the earth, and the trees and rocks.

Music brought them close. It was the peace and the courage that graced every moment, every memory.

They sang their own melody to the Pagan prayer to Mother Earth:

> "You indeed are duly called great Mother o' the gods; you conquer by your divine name. You are the source of the strength of nations and of gods, without you nothing can be brought to perfection or be born. You are the great queen of the gods. Goddess!"[2]

As the women's melody grew softer and their strides shorter, their sacks grew heavier. Nan began wondering aloud, as she often did as the spirits spoke to her. "There is an evil lurking close. Closer than we have imagined," Nan told Saren. "An evil that gains power and momentum from mans' greed," Nan stopped upon the path at the edge of the road. Taking Saren's arm, she looked upon her. "It is the greed of the Church that I am telling you of. Their greed for power and money. Perhaps your father is right that the people must hear the word of God in their own language." Nan continued her march homeward, saying, "We must help him, then. He is doing good to share these books. Come."

The aged woman hurried their steps.

CHAPTER THREE

Past Windsor

Lord Percy was in route to Windsor to witness the farewell of King Richard's entourage venturing across the Irish Sea. Though eager to return north, The Lord kept his focus on the celebrations at hand, knowing a much grander celebration would come with a new king upon the horizon. The sacred book would soon be his, giving him great power and ensuring Henry Bolingbroke would be his pawn. Lord Percy could not help but smile.

An emerald spring welcomed the council to Windsor. Morning revealed a pristine crimson sunrise as they marched toward the coast. Travel was swift and comfortable in the warm, dry weather. Charles carried his pipes loose across his back, atop his bow and quiver, ready to retrieve them quickly. His blade, heavy and awkward, clanked against his thigh.

Charles marched onward, nearly oblivious to the day, for his thoughts remained back at his cottage with his daughter and her grandmamma. With a heavy sigh, he tried to concentrate on his steps upon the aged Roman road.

"Pipe up, Charles. What has got your mind a-wondering?" Thomas, Charles's fellow knight and comrade, inquired.

"Whew, Oh Thomas. Ah, dinnae ken. I have a dreadful notion of this expedition. Tensions are heightened with our leaders this day. Though the sun is warm. I do feel a storm on the horizon," Charles said through a forced smile.

The regiment arrived at Windsor with abundant provisions as well as men. King Richard's council came some days later. A tournament was set for St. George's Day, where the grassy meadow was crowded with knights and squires all dressed in green. The patrons, though, were only those who would embark to Ireland: The Duke of Surrey's company of 100 men and 800 archers and the Dukes of Albermarle and Exeter, each with nearly 700 men. The Earls of Gloucester, Salisbury, and Worcester brought regiments almost as large as the North's.[3]

The gathering in Windsor was intended for splendor and festivities. Still, after the brief exchange of opinions around Lord Percy's campfire on the road, Charles could not help but see the apparent desperation growing. The power to control appointments to office or the right to privileges was completed by the arrival of the Earl of Westmorland and his council. The next day, all parties gathered to witness the King's public farewell to his young niece, Elizabeth. Queen Anne had passed months prior. King Richard escorted his niece amid the courtyard gardens. They strolled, taking deliberate steps as they spoke. Of course, no other would hear what words were spoken, though they seldom shared a smile with all the eyes that befell them.

As they reached the courtyard's center, King Richard lifted his niece from her tiny feet into his embrace for all to see. Covering her angelic face in an array of feathery kisses, he promised her that she would join him in Ireland. Bidding her a final farewell, King Richard smiled and kissed her repeatedly. No smile had ever appeared on her lips that Charles could recognize.

The Earls of Northumberland and Westmorland and their select men did not accompany the glorious parade past Windsor. However, the remaining regiment was simply distinguished. King Richard set sail for Ireland as late May winds blew, with fifty-six ships, 576 commandeered horses, and as many men-at- arms, archers, churchmen, and lords. [4]

A new moon taunted the late May sky, where wisps of clouds hurried to hide its silhouette. The smell of wet grass and damp earth hinted at a new day's dawning.

Charles switched from playing a jig to playing ballads. Repositioning his pipes upon his shoulder, he changed the melody as his mood shifted with the foreseeable consequences of the impending voyage.

Lord Percy's departure left a bitter and salty taste upon Charles's tongue that no music flavor would cleanse.

Unaware of his heart's turmoil, his comrades clapped and danced regardless of his ever-shifting music repertoire. "Play us another reel, Charles. We've another fresh dancer here to join the ranks!" his friend James requested.

Charles would play another reel, then another.

With each breath, he questioned his old friend's motives. "Whatever is Percy up to?" Charles asked the sinking moon. "Why did Percy slip away from the camp so soon and silently?" Since the night of Percy's son Henry's request of Saren's presence, his demeanor had been hostile and unfamiliar.

Preparations for departure escalated.

"Thomas let's get our travels underway," Charles declared as he buried his doubts and concerns among provisions within their ship's hull and his pipes away for safekeeping. "The sooner we get this journey started, the sooner we can return safely home."

Soldiers filed onto the ships' newly polished decks, each dressed in military regalia of red with woolen hats.

Armed with polished swords at their hips, the men carried bows with tasseled quivers strapped upon their backs.

The King's knights stood on guard, forming a single row of men before the sentry. Their leaders moved to the front, walking past the knight's front line, and entered the foyer of Conwy castle.

The sun hurried its descent toward the Kingdom of Leinster, their Irish destination.

Thirty-six massive ships with glorious sun-bleached canopies set sail upon the early summer waters. The air lingered sweet, as evidenced by the continual taste upon one's lips. The coolness of the air pressed heavily upon the sea, like the vessels that pushed westward from the Cornish homeland.

The morning of the second dawn, Charles rose to the creaking of the ship's hull. Men and boys roused and prepared the ship's mast. Raging winds fed their strength to the crashing waves below. The waves grew steadily. Each ship, heavily laden with essential provisions and royal extravagance, prepared for its private strife beyond the storm.

Urgent commands from officers took precedence over any morning greetings among the crew. The peaceful Irish expedition had shifted like the storm upon the jagged coast before them.

The ships rocked and creaked to the continual rhythm of crashing water upon water, for each break upon the water's surface was a premonition of the wrath that was to come.

Humbled by the storm, soldiers prayed for their safety. They could do nothing except hold on to the ship's railing or a secure object to avoid being washed overboard.

Secured among the hull, Charles played his pipes in tempo to nature's wrath. He played, his notes loud and fierce above the roar of the water, and he played for his stamina to outlast the roar of heaven's thunder.

As the sun pierced the morning's calm like one ship's slivered mast, the men worked rapidly to remove most supplies to be ferried to shore.

Horses, oxen, hogs, and a few boys enjoyed the swim. One by one, with tools and provisions of dried lentils and meats, each armsman reached the coast of Ireland.

Supplies arrived in haste. The first of the plenitude to be ushered ashore was celebrating. Before any camp or order was set, endless merrymaking began about having landed on solid ground from the storm. Charles, too, partook of the generous King's abundance. On the next sunrise, however, he and a few other armed men attempted to create order by corralling and collecting the loose livestock and rationing food—which was futile.

That day, the Irish chieftains came to meet the English. The wild Irish portrayed themselves as uncivilized in rebuke to King Richard's previous attempts to rule them.

The chieftains arrived at the camp wearing cow halters made of hemp around their necks, naked and barefoot as if they were criminals, and knelt before King Richard, displaying humility—however false the humility of the Irish would later prove to be.

This submissive welcome from the people that they had arrived to conquer fueled the soldiers' festive spirit. Where the drinking and frolicking prevailed, all strength and discipline waned.

Charles played his pipes each morning to wake the men, and each morning, once they awoke, the festivities would soon follow. No command was issued or obeyed.

Food and supplies grew thinner, and broth and bread became the expected ration. Charles, one of the first to realize that the rations were dwindling, took heed. And as the shortages became apparent among the men, food disappeared more rapidly.

The Irish became friendlier as the English grew hungry. Daily ventures into Dublin became a simple thirty-minute jaunt for the deprived. With the jolly welcome and generous donations of mead from the Irish, the visiting Englishmen continued their festivities.

Weeks passed, and Charles habitually sat near the busy trail to the city to play his pipes. Here, he noticed men lurking in the trees. He sat, frozen, as three Irishmen surrounded his comrade approaching upon the trail and slit his throat with a blade. They dragged the warm body aside, hiding it in a shallow ditch.

Charles dared not move. Instead, he sat frozen upon the stone earth, waiting to slip unseen into the night. No stars dared show their faces to the hideous noise that the night brought forth. Before Charles could slip unnoticed into the shadows, a lone English sailor strolled unexpectedly toward his end.

Charles's large frame was too massive to move in rapid warning, though he swiftly moved his hollow pipes to his lips and played. The percussion of the waves upon the shoreline accompanied his serenade, his music lingering in the air; he watched the lad walk unscathed beyond the attackers. Charles could not afford to be the victim of such an ambush and quickly rushed beyond the hills and back to camp to report his observations.

Word spread rapidly at the English camp, and the missing were tallied. Sunrise loomed, and the lad seen leaving alone upon the trail was counted among the murdered.

Weeks had become months. The untrained militia ran short of food and began to beg, steal, fight, and riot among themselves. King Richard requested a truce with the Irish chieftain MacMurrough. MacMurrough, though, remained indignant that the King of England would dare relocate upon his shore, and small groups of Irish fighters continued to harass the English with sly attacks.

No agreement or terms were made with MacMurrough. King Richard grew pale with anger, swearing, "By St. Edward, I will never depart from Ireland till I have MacMurrough in my clutches."

With a bounty of 100 marks upon MacMurrough's head, King Richard organized his men, sharpened their blades', and organized a march on Dublin.

The stars did not show their faces. The fires burned brightly. The waves broke below to their own rhythm to the tune of nature.

Anger fueled the fight for every man. The sword was nothing more than a heavy burden to Charles. Sharp. It could be sharper, but he might be compelled to use it. Worse yet, he may fall, impelling it through his own flesh.

Soldiers encircled the flames, each sharpening his weapon. The music of Charles's breath filled their ears.

The fear of death is a powerful force upon a man's mind. All eyes awaited the starlight overhead as Charles played his music to the tempo of the crashing waves below. His muscles were primed to run when death beckoned. He grew nearer to the grave with each turning of the tide. Charles awakened to the new day and found brief victory in surviving the night, yet the urgency to flee and hide was honest.

Hiding his fear each day behind his pipes, he played his tune. Only he knew his veiled dread of battle. His time drew nearer; this he understood. Though courage, he had but a dull blade and a song to give.

"Those I fight, I do not hate. Those I fight for I do not love." Charles sang the melody of a well-known tune through his pipes.

The foul weather and the ill talk among the men proved that the peaceful expedition to find alliance with the Irish took a hostile turn weeks before the moment the English ships set sail from Wales.

The Englishmen were dressed in hard leather helmets, some wearing chainmail strapped across their chests. The remaining horses carried the King and his closest allies, all dressed in metal armor displaying high rank. Hunger was now the Englishmen's driving force, fueling them on to Dublin.

The early morning cooled as rains threatened from the sea. Fears and dread among the men were muffled and dissuaded as encouraging words showered from the knights riding upon the horses. "Pottage and mead await us in Dublin, among eager young women for your pleasures," one mounted armsman yelled as they neared the city's edge.

The gang of English stormed side by side across the city's threshold. Yet their strength waned from the long march with empty stomachs. The Irish diverted the English aggression as the militia entered the city. Small bands of Irish penetrated the English front line, disbanding and diluting the force, killing many and wounding more. The casualties were overwhelming. Those who remained uninjured retreated to their meager camp upon the shore. They raced back to the shore one by one, each man for himself, with no order among the frightened.

Their fires hissed and popped. They could have heard footsteps upon the rocks if they were alert enough to listen, as they were continually pursued by the Irish through the night.

Charles rolled in his slumber. He woke to the growl of his stomach or perhaps the sound of hunger from the sleeping man nearby. Neither moonlight nor starlight pierced the sea's steam. Nothing coerces a man from his doze like the voices of a foreign tongue.

Charles rolled closer to the sleeping soldier. He laid his palm over the other man's lips and spoke as softly as his thundering heart allowed. "Shh. Get your weapon. Wake the others. They're upon us."

Grabbing his pipes, he crawled to another sleeping man. Then another. Unfamiliar words cackled through the darkness.

Sweat collected atop Charles's mopped head of hair despite the coolness before the dawn. He licked his cracked lips and spotted one final sleeping soldier lying prone.

Chatter and sounds of urgency arose from the camp on the shore. Charles unsheathed his sword from a kneeling position and rose. The silhouette of the budding moon was all that remained to witness this wrath of man. The approaching screams of attack drowned the muffled cries of the men and boys under siege.

"Charles, carrying his blade at his side, ran to his remaining comrades. Charles's haste bred further urgency among his friends. The morning had broken. The warriors pushed past and around, preventing Charles from reaching the front line of the ambush. Charles froze there in battle. His dull weapon dropped like clay. His breath gushed past his dry lips as the thud-thud of his heart's beat echoed within his skull. The haze of the encroaching dawn imploded upon him as his vision became dim. A foreign blade pierced his heart, and a warm, moist pool of blood now saturated his woolen tunic. He felt no pain until the blade was extracted with a screech and a massive heave.

His great form became an obstacle for those who hustled in desperate defense.

Charles's massive body, now useless, remained among the fixtures on the beach. His energy raged like the coast waters, like a frequency unique to Charles's soul that continued unburdened now by the body's heavy form. A spirit freed and unique as the stars above.

The cloth wrapped around Charles's waist lay smooth and straight. The weight of worn wool no longer rippled in the wind. The black and green of the woven plaid had blended from constant exposure to the elements. The patterned crimson squares faded to pink, adding contrast and depth to the thinner bars of color. The rosy hues of Charles's kilt and the peach of his skin did nothing to soften the striking color of his ginger beard, long and curly. The only alarming disruption to the man's appearance was his lifeless body.

Though the aggression of the Irish was successful, word came of the King's contender, Henry Bolingbroke's arrival in England. By the end of this summer's day, King Richard began a hasty pilgrimage back across the Irish Sea.

◆   ◆   ◆

Love is a powerful force in the hearts of men. Love conquers greed and envy. Love comforts and soothes. Love is never cruel or destructive. Love, the strongest of energies, can exist forever.

Charles played his pipes through this war zone because of the love that remained in his heart.

His spirit rose, inspecting his surroundings, leaving his weapon, useless as it was, sleeping on the earth. Out of habit, he ducked and dodged riots, missed jabs and clubs by a breath. He reclaimed his pipes. A stone behind him guarded his back. He poured the music from his life. Notes of his being and from his soul. He played to drown each warrior's scream of death.

CHAPTER FOUR

Saren's Promise

"Mother Earth takes care of us all when we take care of her," Nan sang as she crouched at the shore, cleaning the refuse from the fresh-caught salmon. "The season is plentiful. We must smoke all that we catch for our winter's provisions." She stacked the bounty of their day's catch upon the stone. "Saren, girl. Fuel the fire strong—we need more kindling."

Saren leaped to the task. As sparse as wood was inland, planks, kelp, and debris washed there upon the shore, making the beach a prized location for gathering firewood. The girl hunted and gathered wood to feed their flame.

The sun shone brightly upon them, hardly warm, as summer slowly escalated. Saren stepped barefoot along the pebbled beach, searching for fuel and treasures to call her own.

Jewels and gems were the treasures of most children, but Saren was no longer a child and now thought more of survival than play as she searched for the perfect bone to fashion a bow, or the perfect stone to fashion a blade.

The marble-like stone she found washed up on the shore shimmered darker than other rocks, which caught her eye. Rocks she had found before were often dark but never as black as this—like a moonless night, black as an empty expanse of nothing. She smoothed her thumb upon the glass-like surface. *It is not glass,* she pondered, holding its razor edge gingerly. Saren returned to the fire to help her Nan and ask how to turn this mysterious treasure into a blade.

Nan's whalebone handle that she had been fashioning supported the stone blade as though nature had designed them to match. Saren then wrapped the joint with sinew to avoid any slippage. Feeling surreal in her grip, she smiled as she nodded, satisfied. The blade was razor sharp, and the stone was never cold. Proud of her creation, Saren shared in its construction with her grandmamma. Though longing for her father's presence to witness this small success, Saren mourned his absence.

"I long for Father," she said, looking into the dying embers of their fire. "I regret our quarrels over me marrying, now." She took a deep breath of the smoky air and added, "I don't regret not agreeing to the betrothal, no. But I wish that I had not argued so."

"Marriage is a beautiful union, Child when a husband and wife are joined by the most powerful force, love." Nan sighed, shutting her sparkling eyes to the bright sun or perhaps to the sweet memory of loves long departed. "Be ever cautious, too, my child. Love is a tricky and treacherous emotion often made a game by those evil enough to have greed as their motive."

Saren nodded in agreement. "Lord Percy's son does not love me at all, Nan. Why, I've never seen him with my own two eyes." Saren returned to smoothing her treasured knife.

"There is plenty of time, my child, for love to find you. Your season is not yet ripe, and as I have told him often, your father knows that you are not ready to bear a man's fruit, as wea a lass as you be." The old woman hugged her granddaughter close as Saren clung to her weapon in one hand. They rocked to and fro in tempo to the gentle waves' rhythm upon the shore.

"What motive, do you reckon, has Sir Percy in me, Nan? He has never seen my person and the little royal lineage I have of Eadioune is of Pict descent. Is it not? So, what is his motive?" Saren whipped her skirt about her in dismay.

"Darling girl. You've plenty to share, no doubt," Nan unfurred her creasing brow. "You also have your father's treasured book," she added.

They discussed the marriage proposal no further, sharing only the silent knowing and understanding shared by two souls. Their love would withstand the test of time.

"The sun is our life and our restoration. We trust that it appears each day to bring us warmth and leaves each night to bring us safety and rest," Nan began her hymn to the heavens. She sang softly, raising her pitch as the tide returned to grace the coast. Saren, having heard the chant since she was in her mother's womb, sang along:

"And he led them in a cloud by day and all the night by a fiery light." [5]

Father had been away for weeks. He had been expected home days ago. Saren had not been concerned with why he had not yet returned. "Worries are nothing but wasted thoughts," Nan had reminded her as the moon waxed upon the horizon's edge. Saren and Grand Mamma meandered the coastline for more wood for their fire.

Walking hand in hand, they had not yet found more kindling. Instead,

Nan walked on, telling of the moon's powers upon the tides and their lives.

The bound book remained hidden, tucked neatly in Saren's treasure chest beneath her newest pinafore. She dared not touch the secret book, for it radiated impending action. Each day, each moment that passed without her father's return, brought her ever closer to having to fulfill her promise.

The candle was lit while the women ate a meager dinner of boiled root and greens. The fish smoked beyond the house's wall would be saved for winter.

Trouble rumbled upon the western seaside, and just as darkness consumed their home, Saren spoke of her plans to Nan. "I have the secret book, Nan, that Father entrusted to me. The time is near that I ought to deliver it to London for safekeeping."

Nan jumped to her feet, hurrying around the kitchen, cursing the darkness about her. "Nay, my girl. We shall remain here for safekeeping. As should the book of your father's." At last, Nan returned to her chair. Tears welled behind her lashes. Taking Saren's hand in hers, she added, "I know, Lass. I'm angry this family's curse has fallen on you." She wiped the trickling tears away. "I wish I were young again and would go with you." The elderly women stooped to coddle Saren's shimmering black curls.

As Saren lay upon her straw mattress, they did not talk anymore that night. She would not press the issue with her dear Grandmamma. However, she planned to fashion a bow tomorrow. Arrows, she had plenty.

The welcome celebration was short and bittersweet for Saren. Lord Percy and his elite men returned in full regalia this day to Northumberland, for they had not taken the Irish voyage with the others. The sun burned shallow in the western sky.

Fathers, brothers, and sons did not return from the Irish expedition. However, the question about Lord Percy was whispered upon each breath. Why had he not accompanied his king across the Irish Sea while so many others had?

Saren's troubled heart beat a rhythm out of the tempo of her thoughts. Her agitation rose with the tide, and her countless questions fueled her haste. Like the waves, her doubts grew. She knew as well as Nan that her father could only answer her questions, and he had not returned. There was a reason for Lord Percy's premature return, and Saren, certain of her plight, grew ever anxious to find answers about her father's whereabouts.

Only one other soul could answer her questions and calm her troubled mind. Saren set out at once to speak to Lord Percy himself.

Ale was passed among the Percy's men. The celebration grew more intense the deeper Saren stepped into the crowd. Had her father returned among these men? Perhaps then she might have a reason for cheer. Though so many remained abroad, the elite of the Northumberland regiment had only returned. No Irish soil had graced their feet.

Chatter was plentiful among the men. Saren's questions to the men fell upon deaf ears. An elderly lord took heed and gave Saren a nod to speak to Lord Percy.

"My Lord, may I request your company for a moment?" Saren asked with awkward cheer. She had grown from a child with this lord's presence nearby. He had sat around her father's table and sipped her father's ale. He shared stories and sorrows with her family and hers with his. Her father had called him a friend for decades. She said again, "Lord Percy, it is I, Saren."

Lord Percy appeared to look beyond her. No smile graced his lips. The celebrated lord peered at his friend's daughter as though she were no one that he cared to know.

"It is I, my lord, Saren Eadwine, daughter of Charles. May I ask, Lord Percy, why my father did not return home with you this day?" Saren looked directly into his gaze. Before she finished her question, she knew from the man's expressionless face that he would not tell her what she desperately wanted to know. The empty eyes told her far more than his lying words would ever. She knew in a silent instant that he, Lord Percy of Northumberland, had deceived her father. Why else would he not have followed the royal fleet abroad? And above all, *why has he returned home?* she thought.

She was flushed from the heat and wiped sweaty palms across her skirt. Saren caught his gaze for one more moment and stepped within a whisper's breath of his face. She spoke, "You know more than you tell. My father, your friend, is a way to gain an alliance with the wild Irish for what? To return home to fight a battle not to be won, or to not return home?" Saren hesitated. Her words carried a heavy weight that she now understood. His gaze remained lifeless yet menacing. "You deceived my father and have taken him from me for what profit to you?" Saren asked and walked past his black eyes, knowing that no words from his deceiving lips would console her.

Saren turned to leave in haste. Unwilling to waste another breath upon such a traitor as Lord Percy, she hastened away, but he grasped her arm. Jerking her to a stop, he spun her about to face him, his eyes penetrating her to the core. Any friendly tone left his voice as he whispered for only her ears to hear, "I know what your father has left to your safekeeping, child."

She pulled free from his grasp and turned to leave without causing any further commotion.

As she walked away, she could feel Lord Percy's words slap her back as he said, "Child. The rightful heir has come home to regain his throne."

His words clawed at the back of her skull as she hurried away. She dared not turn and ask him to clarify his meaning. She had heard what he said and now knew that Lord Percy had also betrayed King Richard.

Saren slept in fits. She woke before dawn before questions of her departure could arise. Having slept in her clothes, she needed little preparation to leave. The book of her fathers was bound, though the red seal with the intricately circled eight-point star had been opened. Saren kept her promise, braided her ebony hair, and fled to deliver her family's secret book to Jon the Mute at London's city center. No time was left for fashioning a bow.

Lord Percy's words smoldered in her ears. The urge to run overwhelmed her. Father had told her she must deliver the book to London if he did not return. She would not taste food this day.

Father was not coming home. Too many moons had come and gone for the soldier to return. Saren prepared for the inevitable. She wanted desperately to explain her rapid departure to Nan.

Her grief hastened her. She gathered her few possessions, laced them in her satchel with her father's secret book and other forbidden bibles secured beneath her bosom, and fled silently.

All she owned, she carried—her knife, clothes, map, a small bit of freshly smoked haring with the memories of her life. Her love for her home and her father would remain secure in her heart where no one could pilfer it.

Clutching her arm across her breast, she held tightly to her satchel. Saren hurried on, away from the village's candles. She climbed the west ridge outside the town, away from the coast, the direction that insurgence or French allies might emerge. Silhouetted against the morning haze, Saren found several fallen trees on the ground. She sat, removed her pack, and rested.

Looking to the village below for reassurance, only memories of Nan remained there for her to mourn. No father would return. Saren wept to the silent morning as she ate bits of the wheat loaf, she had purchased days ago. The brittle bread had been her last reassurance from the town. *How can I, just a girl, keep these sacred books away from the Earl of Northumberland?* She thought. Saren sat upon a fallen tree, watching, and listening to the morning.

A gentle breeze blew in from the ocean. Pigeons cooed to one another, not comprehending that they, too, were amid war. They called a melody of goodness that brought a smile to her lips, the first in days. "I'd best move on," she said aloud. After one last glance and with a steady stride, Saren left the fallen trees.

Cresting the adjacent ridge, she turned to what she imagined were shouts from afar. Seeing nothing, she prayed, "Sorry, my Nan. Peace is with you, and my love." She turned from the promise of daybreak and pressed south.

Reluctant and careful, she crept closer to the edge of the neighboring hamlet. There were no lamps lit, no carts or people in the streets. Only the lonely look of a deserted town. Saren stole in, following the edge of the worn street.

"Hello, town. I come in peace," Saren warned the fronts of stone buildings. No response answered her. Saren marched down the cobbled road, her head high and shoulders back. She moved toward the water well close to the village center. Near this, she located a welcoming barn.

And refuge as well, though she did not know that King Richard's oppressors had already landed upon English soil and had just begun their campaign, with Lord Percy beside them and searching for her.

No breeze yet wafted in from the coast, leaving a cloak of fog lingering across the land. Nan woke before dawn before enough light could penetrate the air.

Stillness rested upon the house, such a quiet she had once grown accustomed to as a child when she was left all alone. And here now, this recognition sent surges of panic through her heart. She called, "Saren, child, are you here?"

Slipping from her mattress, she called again, "Saren, please tell me you're about, girl." She grabbed her shawl and strode from one stone wall to the opposite to confirm her worst suspicions.

She was alone. Rushing to the remaining candle, she sat as tears filled her heavy, dark eyes. Refusing to allow them to fall, she set a flame upon the kindling and steeped her morning tea as she donned her worn and tattered garments for the day.

With a heavy heart, she rushed to her granddaughter's chest. There, beneath her new white dress, the bound forbidden book was gone.

Saren had slept again in her clothes. Her boots lay in a heap on the dirt floor. Awakening, she reached for them, hesitating to rub the soles of her feet before slipping the aged and brittle leather on and lacing them. Her stomach rumbled in response to the tangy scent of a roasting rabbit. Saren pushed the great door open, hunting for the aroma's source, but the smell was lost beyond the barn's walls. "Where are your cooking fires?" Saren asked the rafter above. The walls didn't reply. Saren sniffed the heavy air again and determined the scent was coming from behind the stone barn. There was no opening for light, so she inched along the stone wall, feeling her way. At the far reaches of the barn, a small gate stood open to allow a sliver of sunlight to trickle down to the ground. *Why are there no animals?* Saren wondered. *Trust no one.* She reminded herself.

Saren raised her trembling hand to brush away the cobwebs from her face. She breathed a deep and slow breath of the dusty air and listened.

A fire popped and hissed beyond the door. Saren wiped her dirty hands on her skirt, tried to speak, and then stopped to listen. She could hear no voices from inside the barn. Saren slipped behind a hay crate, pressing flush to the wall, and she listened on. Lying motionless on the wooden planks, staring up at the glistening flecks of dust that danced in the air. The only light coming through came from the door she had wiggled ajar.

The sun ceased to grace the dancing dust about her and had sunk down upon the western horizon; Saren rolled to her stomach and crawled across the aged wood toward the cracked door. The snapping and hissing of the fire drowned out any other sound. She crept closer to the light. No voices came. Only the salty scent of meat. Saren's stomach moaned, and her mouth watered in protest. She placed her open hands across her middle to muffle the noise. Closing her eyes, she prayed. "My Lord, my God. Thank you for leading me here safely. Forgive my temptations."

Saren pulled herself up from the sanctuary of the feed bunk and peered around the stone walls of the barn. The fire smoldered beneath a tall iron spit straddling the flames. A prominent figure stood near, ladling broth over the sizzling hare. Saren pulled her gaze away and retreated to the refuge of her hiding place. She waited.

The meat sizzled and popped over the fire. Saren lay on the bottom of the feed bunk as the day wore on. The massive hulk of a man, whom she had heard humming an unfamiliar tune, was no friend but a wolf among the scavengers. Saren closed her eyes to hide from his image or his gaze. She waited in the trough for moonlight to seep through the cracked door.

Eventually, the fire no longer hissed beyond the wall as she raised her weary body. Saren stepped with purpose and determination that can be fueled only by an empty stomach. The fire continued to radiate heat from the glowing coals that touched the edge of night. The warmth reached Saren while she slid along the inner wall of the barn. The silence of the night was crushing. No birds sang; no breeze dared blow this smoke that cloaked the heated summer air. Saren crept onward, silent as the night. The spit remained over the fire, and the remains of the hare dangled there. Saren crawled on her belly; her mouth wet in anticipation. She reached for the meat. She couldn't see the man, but she knew he was nearby, for labored and muffled snores rose steadily nearby. Saren removed the meat, every speck that remained. Nibbling a corner, she wrapped her prize in the pinafore of her dress and tied the corners through her belt.

The sleeping foe choked awake. Saren glanced around for anything more that she could take with her.

The scavenger grumbled and woke with a snort. Saren quieted her heart and tried not to move into the smoky haze. Not a breath passed from her lips. Without repose, she waited. The lingering scent of meat in the air brought growls from her stomach. Time was at hand for Saren to flee.

She reached the hiding place where she had spent the day but then went on to the refuge of the hay where she had hidden the hours past dawn. Retrieving her leather satchel, she freed her morsel of meat. After eating enough to quiet her hunger, she tucked the remainder into her pack. Where there remains one foe, others shall appear, she thought. Saren tiptoed back to the village center and to the water well.

Silent like the smoke, she hoisted a bucket from the depth. There was plenty of water to quench her thirst and clean her hands and face. Though wishing she could stay and indulge longer in the water, Saren knew this village had served her well. She dried her face upon her skirt and moved as prey fled from a predator's gaze. Saren scurried toward the edge of the village.

Doors that she passed were left askew. Rubbish and belongings remained behind. There was an appearance to the place that can only come when folks are given just enough time to flee for their lives. The outermost building lay paces away. Saren accepted the horizon to the west, of hills and valleys, to be her destination. Saren hurried on toward London.

A wind swirled from the north, blowing her skirts against her body. She stopped there on the road to adjust the binding wool. The gust receded, and she stood tall before she took another step. A small cry rose from behind the last door—a weak, frail cry, long and piercing like a starving babe.

She saw no choice. She ran toward the cry.

CHAPTER FIVE

Purgatory

The attack was swift, the blows surreal. With every cry of pain, another poor soul was freed. Neither superiority nor judgment was bestowed on the fallen there in battle. No longer immune to death, they, too, bled and died. The young soldier whom Charles played for fought gallantly, holding his ground. Seven Irishmen fell to his sword.

The young soldier alone displayed enough bravery for them both. A faint smile touched Charles's lips, anticipating him finally finding heaven. Lost in himself, Charles had no time to warn the brave soldier of his approaching foe. Charles played on, for he could feel his music more than hear it, and Charles's music rose wild and free, a song of warning.

⬥　　⬥　　⬥

The loneliness became more bearable as Nan prepared her winter's provisions. However, the pleasure of doing so was lost in not having another to share in the season's rituals.

The quiet of the aged-stone home began to comfort the old woman as the endless chatter and muffled snores of loved ones once had. This day, the quiet was playing tricks upon her. She had often risen to locate the drone of Charles's pipe music, and here again, it appeared within the cusp of her quiet. "Charles, I hear you play as close as the day is upon my lids." Nan reached for the shuttered window to peer beyond to where he would sit upon the rocks and sing his pipes to the tide during the summer months long past.

No pipe music played from there this day, but in its place, Nan saw men approaching.

Barring the door behind her, she took her only blade—a cooking blade— and Charles's last remaining Bible and stowed near the well.

The small group of men penetrated her home effortlessly. They gave no warnings and made no demands.

The stone remained secure and solid there upon Charles's beach, just a stone forever and formidable to witness the ebb and the flow of this ever-expanding world. Charles remained there playing across the tide as his old friend ransacked his home just beyond his shoulder in search of his family's sacred book, now his daughter's treasure. Charles played on, forbidding Nan from leaving her sanctuary.

Nan prayed and waited. As the men cleared, she remained hidden into the day. Before the heavy night cloak covered her, she feared even lighting a candle. At last, comforted by her soft humming, Nan exited her hiding place.

Everything in the home had been ransacked. Nan caressed her belongings, trying to make right all the men had wronged. She had recognized one or two of the intruders' voices, yes, as Charles's fellow armsmen and counts to Lord Percy.

Nan crumpled to the floor, clutching her torn coat that had been tossed aside. She realized the betrayal that had fallen upon her family. Charles had been summoned away to Ireland, and the timing of Saren's marriage proposal haunted her heart. Nan stood, pulling her damaged coat and heart close, and gathered what provisions she could salvage. Her granddaughter was being hunted; this she knew. The treasures she carried to London were more precious and powerful than all the English Bibles. Lord Percy, his son, and his men would stop at nothing to gain such power.

She closed her eyes to the evil that remained simmering within her home and desperately searched for a candle and mugwort to cleanse the air. Nan knew who the men were, what they sought, and that they would do anything to have their treasure.

Though she was elderly, she was strong, and she was able. Nan knew where Saren had fled and that she was in danger. The old woman's love for her granddaughter hastened her away to warn her.

CHAPTER SIX

A Warning Heard

The waves kept their rhythm against the pull of the moon. The sun made its appearance and then retreated of its own accord.

Charles marched along the beach, his stamina never wavering, his muscles never aching.

Frustrated by his solitude, he sat aimlessly, watching the remaining morning stars battle the sun for more time, a battle never to be won. His loneliness was as vast as the sea before him, and he had no company but the stars.

No tears could fall to match his sorrow. No salty air, though all around, did he taste. Just the empty void of a wandering soul remained.

Charles marched again, through nights and beyond. The jagged coast surrounded him as he traveled. Neither pain nor desolation could reach him now, and with a tempo of revenge, he stepped on. Resting his great frame— now only a cool breeze of spirit light—as the sun hinted of dawning, Charles climbed atop a slick stone to witness the awakening of the day. He played his pipes.

Charles played for the morning stars. Charles played for the wind from the sea, and he played for any listening ear that might hear. It was a flawless tone, without blemish and without refrain. Charles played of his love for his daughter, a pure and sweet melody, a song like his unconditional love, without beginning and without end. His song grew heavy like his heart, filled with remorse and determination. Charles filled his pipes bellow for the rising of the sun. He stood and marched into the sunrise to find his Saren, whom he had given world- changing secrets to bear. What dread had Charles passed on to his only child, this dread his family had carried for generations? He could not let her carry such secrets in his place. His purpose was now to return to Saren and to help protect her and the family's book with unwavering resolve.

He marched now with a purpose because somewhere in the night, Saren slept alone and was probably frightened. She lived without her father. Loneliness was her companion for this journey he had granted her.

Saren still lived. This Charles knew. He could not know where she traveled, nor could he find her. His trial to help her and find bravery must be completed on this path before he can see his journey to heaven.

His worn leather sole gripped the damp stone of the shore. A moist breeze from the sea would have brought the smell of salt and ocean life if someone were near to smell it. Hesitating a breath, Charles noticed that he had arrived on English soil. The need to travel, to press on, consumed his spirit. He must hurry now to reach his countrymen, Saren, and warn the kingdom of the approach of Henry Bolingbroke's French and now English rebels from Wales. The warning would be quick and sharp, a fierce cry of urgency, a warning salute that all would recognize, that would fulfill his duties here to this sovereign King. The urgency of his mission was palpable.

The volume of voices and animals at Market Bosworth woke him from his trance. He could hear carts' wheels, shouts, and clopping hooves before the city was in view. No soldiers were poised to meet the coming attack. Charles drew close to the city, listening to the joy of the unsuspecting inhabitants laughing and moving through their summer mornings, unprepared for war. Charles stepped across the city street, tall and proud, to warn the innocent city of their King's fate and perhaps their own.

Alive with the bustle and clamor of life, the city stank of animal refuse and human waste. Rains had penetrated the streets and washed the filth into pools of decay that encouraged even the spirits to hurry past.

By the Bosworth's gates, there was a dark jungle of buildings. Loud and omnipresent, the city pressed down around Charles's spirit, dank and riddled with grime.

He stepped toward a man, raised his hand to his mouth, and cleared his throat. "Prepare your men. I have come from the coast. Bolingbroke's ships are approaching from the south," Charles spoke.

The tall, bearded man wiped his face, furrowed his brow, and walked on. Refusing to accept the man's ignorance, Charles approached another, stopping a feather's width from his lips. Charles spoke again, "Bolingbroke's men will be here by nightfall. Prepare yourselves!" The man's eyes widened, and he wiped his face clean, sensing Charles's presence, and stepped to the side and around him. He, too, walked away without acknowledgment.

Fury seized him. Charles ran to the nearest cart and clambered atop the many crates. He stood tall and shouted to the dozens of passersby, "People, listen here. I have come to warn you. Hurry. Prepare yourselves!"

No one turned. No one looked toward Charles as he shouted his words of warning. He could not make them hear him. No matter how many times he tried, he could not push a crate from the loaded wagon.

Alas, he sat fixating on the forces and winds around him to propel the heavy cart upon the earth. The crash caught onlookers' attention, and a crate nearly fell on an elderly woman. People gasped and looked his way. Charles shouted his warnings again. The mess was swept away. The old woman was helped to her feet, and men reloaded the crate beside him, but no one could hear his warning. Charles leaped to the ground and strolled through the buzz of people. He watched people making the day's preparations for their lives, their happy lives. He found the blacksmith's shop where weapons could be made. No weapons had been cast of the iron this day, only wheels and tools for tomorrow's use.

A beautiful maiden strolled the edge of the lewd street toward him, white hair spilled to brush her pale skin. Charles watched her approach. She was cast in serene hues of being that followed her every step. Charles's breath was lost as she stopped before him. No words escaped his lips. He stared there in her radiant presence. She leered.

The dark angel spoke a dialect of proximate English.

She told her name, "Mercia is my chosen title."

Enchanted by her beauty, Charles smiled his boyish grin and said, ""My Lady of Light, why do you speak when no other will acknowledge my plea?"

"We are of a contrasting realm, you and I, my Lord." She passed her arms through the air between them and sighed. "This is not a place to remain." She spoke without moving her lips.

"How can we warn the innocent? Little time remains to flee." Charles looked among the unsuspecting faces. "Why are they not alarmed?" He asked.

"That is not your purpose, Charles, son of Eadwine, to warn the people. Warning the innocent, the meek is not why you remain," Mercia said, looking through Charles's eyes into tomorrow but saying no more.

"How can I make them hear me?" he asked the heavens.

Without force or ability to help the poor, unaware souls. *I know what is going to happen that day. A massacre…*

Charles thought as he wiped his knuckles across his nose and avoided meeting the unknowing gazes of passersby. He looked to his boots instead. Charles spoke to the dirt, "I have traveled many days and nights to arrive here in this kingdom. I know what is to become of these people. I have seen what is to follow. What am I to do? Stand and watch the massacre?" Charles threw his arms to the pale sky, swinging his pipes loose from his shoulder.

"Precisely. Charles, son of Eadwine. That is why I have arrived," Mercia confessed. Her eyes were wild in anticipation, and her wet lips glistened. The warmth of her glow was just an illusion. Charles stepped away.

"You know what is going to happen this day? A massacre. Are you eager to witness this?" Charles wiped his soiled knuckles across his nose and avoided meeting this devil angel's gaze. He looked to his boots again. "You know these things, my Lady?" He folded his hand together before his chest as if to pray. "I cannot reach these people." He closed his eyes before he looked away from her gaze.

"You have much to learn, My Lord." Mercia reached for his pipes, but Charles pulled away from her grasp. "Oh," she ceased reaching. "I see. You don't want my help. Of course, it is always best to learn your own path." Mercia walked into the crowded street, turned, and spoke over her shoulder. "How do you know it is these people who will fall and not your precious King?" She cackled. "Charles, son of Eadwine, let it be known you may walk the beaches of Wales for eternity."

Mercia took a moment to let this knowledge find its home before she continued, "Time is nothing here, as the lineal continuation it once was." Mercia turned and left Charles, following her only with his eyes.

"Eternity? That is nonsense," he cursed from pinched lips.

"I left my brothers in battle all but a day ago on the beach. "Touching his head and then his side where no pain could be remembered. Charles made his way to the edge of the civilized perimeter. The people would have a place to escape from there. Here, he attempted to tell passersby to run, to leave. No one would hear his warning.

"Nothing remains for me, and my daughter now must fight in my place," Charles told the people as if they could hear.

Though trouble smoldered within his breast, he was compelled to leave his thoughts. Charles spat in the dust again, clenched his fists, and looked around at the surrounding large stone walls. He climbed to the highest point on the wall.

Reaching it effortlessly, Charles rose to his calling. Standing atop the city's wall, he witnessed the Bolingbroke's ships long since landed and soldiers moving swiftly inland. He fell to his knees.

"What can I do, my God? I cannot sit idly by and watch as death consumes these helpless souls. Bolingbroke's army has landed, and they have secured support to ambush King Richard's regiment here."

Charles rose to the task before him. Sweat should have been gracing his weary head. He wiped his dry brow, though only out of habit now, and sat upon the wall, resting his massive hands in his lap; hands that seldom would sit idle. Charles reached for his pipes of bone. He could yell no more. He cleared his throat and played his pipes. His chanter played the melody, and the drone kept constant harmony.

Charles poured his heart into the loud bone instrument with a soul- consuming ballad that all would recognize as the augur of impending doom. Charles played. It was the last remaining thing that he could do. Sorrow and urgency filled his every note. He played on. The tone of his pipes came from beneath the deep reaches of his being. The notes passed from his heart. His eyes closed to this world. He played a melody so real, a tone so alive that it fell upon every whisper within its reach.

Witnesses stopped in their steps. Their gazes looked to the heavens and slowed them from their hurried progress. Voices asked what doom pricked their senses. One lad climbed the wall and stopped his incline just a breath from Charles's shoulder, nearly knocking him backward. Suddenly, Charles opened his eyes.

The commotion below increased in a hurried and certain direction toward his roost. The lad stood atop the wall, scanning the surrounding hills, where he found the King's host approaching. Charles watched as the youthful glow of the lad's face turned to a pale shade of stone. The boy shouted what he had seen back to the people below, his voice fearful to announce his finding. Another man joined him on the ledge, scanning the reach to the west. He yelled a late warning to the masses that an army marched on them. Charles leaped from his wall, put his hornpipe to his lips, and walked toward the hope of freedom. Playing liberty's song, the music of Charles's brave soul filled the people's ears. They would follow.

The ships had touched the English coast; blood had spilled upon King Richard's crest. The church doors were left ajar where life had been destroyed.

The laughter of the oppressor filled the Holy house with its deafening roar; Charles ventured in.

The men, both young and old, destroyed everything that was not sacred to them. Two captive men of the cloth remained bound for their entertainment.

Perhaps these were the few of King Richard's court members who had not crossed over to join Bolingbroke. Charles knew that they had chosen righteousness over conformity.

Charles attempted to cast his gaze away as one Holy man's eyes met and locked. "You can see me?" Charles's lips moved to the words, but no sound came. He approached the bloody prisoner.

Kneeling before him, Charles bowed his head and touched his bound wrists.

"Forgive me, Father. I am too late." He raised his head to the priest to see tears falling from his eyes. He spoke gently, "You are not late, my son, but right on time." As Charles knelt nearby, the churchman spoke through the sorrow, torment, and pain.

He could not fight these men, nor could he free the prisoners. But he could fill their souls with a song of righteousness. He played.

The night fell upon them as if to hide the slaughtered innocent. Charles's tunes of love drove the intruder's roars of laughter from the ruins. He played long into the night, filling the Holy walls of the house with a protective present, leaving little room for the ravaging evil to remain.

The heavy doors were shut to no one yet open only for those who could withstand the divine presence that Charles created with his music.

With a subtle pause of rhythm, Charles opened his eyes toward the captive man beside him. His head dipped forward, and his moans ceased. Here, at last before him, the man of God's soul was freeing.

Charles walked among the wounded, playing a song of hope and life to feed their souls like a prayer. Stumbling once upon a notion, he ceased his tune to look up. Mercia was there in her resplendent doom.

"How dare you, woman, to follow me here," he spat. A smile crossed her brow as she spoke. "We travel, my dear Charles, in the same circles. You and I."

Charles shook his red hair. "Perhaps, the same destination, Woman. But we are summoned by foes."

"Aye, you learn fast, Jacob, son of Eadwine," Mercia stepped toward a moaning man lying prone among the broken. She reached forth to touch him as Charles pushed her. The strength of his blow did nothing to detour her touch of the dying man's flesh. Mercia laughed a hideous chuckle of triumph. "Your brute force, dear Charles, is no match for the evils walking among the shadows of death," she cackled again, all the while keeping her open palm upon the man's chilled body.

Chares lowered his bone pipes from his shoulder and closed his eyes so as not to witness Mercia's rape and pillage. Charles played to drown the evil of her laugh from being heard. He played, though weeping.

Time passed unchecked. His eyes had not opened while the moon climaxed, then sank again. On he sang of love through the bone pipes. No urgency nor passion woke him from this trance; he played.

Charles leaped to attention and gasped, "What," He stammered while closing his eyes briefly. "Why do you remain here in my Lord's house, Mercia?"

"Because, my dear Charles, son of Eadwine. You ceased your song and left the door open just for me." She sneered a delighted smile, much like that of a ravenous wolf discovering a fallen stag. "Now, I may continue my feast of heavenly souls." She eyed the hollowed figure of a man who stooped before her. Reaching to grasp his head, she turned to speak.

Chares swung and pushed with all the power of his presence. He raged and fumed at Mercia's indecency, "Your beauty is your daggers, and your laughter your sword."

Charles could do nothing to remove her physical presence away from the Holy House, away from the Holy Man.

Mercia's smile was dangerous. The evil around her shone in the night. "You must leave, my Lord son of Eadwine. You could not bear to watch me take this gentle soul for my supper," she leered.

Mercia reached for his pipes of bone, trying to push his instrument from his grasp. She protested in rage, "Dam Highlander, you learn too well." She covered her ears with her palms and howled to mask Charles's tone. He played on over the man of God, his songs of reckoning. Looking up only once as the night again slowly faded into dawn, he watched the man of the cloth ascend with another honorable soul, who had given Charles a nod of gratitude moments before his soul departed.

CHAPTER SEVEN

Liam

Opening the one door that was purposely closed, not waiting for her eyes to adjust to the blackness of the room and no time to lose, Saren hurried into the ransacked room following the cries.

Stepping into the dwelling, she found an infant beneath its beaten and ashen mother, where no more tears could be spared, only screams of the pain of hunger. "Shhh," Saren crooned as she pulled and twisted the swaddling free from the stiffened corpse of its mother. Wrapping the infant tightly, she clutched him to her breast and fled from the decay that choked the room. The stench was reason enough to hurry on; the baby's cry only increased in volume as they fled.

Saren's meat from the smoking coals was still warm as she knelt among the rocks for cover beyond the town. Here, she could see danger approaching from all but the hillside. Saren sat beneath the stones for protection and peeled back the blood-caked rags holding the tiniest refugee. His cries had ceased long before reaching their shelter. Saren kept traveling with the silent babe long into the night. She thought he slept, but his broad, sunken eyes told otherwise. She wiped her licked thumb across his eyes and mouth to see what response remained. At last, a weak wail erupted, inconsolable by the rocking of Saren's footsteps.

Tearing a morsel from her prized meat, she chewed the meat to form a mushy paste. The child's mouth opened wide in anticipation; she bent to his lips with hers. This was the first infant Saren had ever been so privileged to feed, and she had no milk to give nor the experience to nurse.

Only once the babe cooed and wiggled in delight did Saren eat.

The cloak of night brought needed rest and protection but little sleep for Saren.

No destination awaited them, only Nan to the sorrow of her absence. The two refugees had only each other for physical protection and love. With tomorrow's light, perhaps they would find London. Tonight, Saren thought of the night, so many moons ago, when Joseph read of her Father's secret book upon the Al-Aoura. She thought then of her father. His strong arms held her close. The memory kept her spirits up, but she would never know her father's presence again. Saren cuddled the sleeping child close.

"I shall call you Liam." She lay motionless, watching her little Liam sleep, her mind too full of worry and sorrow for sleep.

Liam dreamed sweet dreams as his tiny fists clenched tightly, and a quiet smile caressed his lips.

Saren sat beneath the false safety of the cold stone, her breathing shallow and filled with haste. She had nothing, yet now everything, to lose.

Her hunger was satisfied for now, as was Liam's. Though hunger is inevitable, knowing it would soon return awakened her instincts.

The value of her life was now surpassed by that of the tiny life she was entrusted with. Her tears would no longer return, for they were of no benefit. Her decisions had led her to this point of no return. She had no roof for shelter and no food. Only forbidden books carrying a forbidden message to share with an unknown priest in unfamiliar London.

The new mother and infant would be out of bread in only a couple days. Their destination then must be toward civilization and where they could find food.

The dawn spilled from the hilltops as birds began to sing. Saren cleaned and fed Liam, wrapped him in her love, and tied him snugly with her other treasures upon her back. She hiked toward London, unaware of the evil that destroyed and ransacked as it pursued her.

The evil Lord Percy and his men had searched for her and her book while she kept hidden long enough in the trough of the old stone barn to escape. Her fortunate timing and quest to save a crying child had proven her grace. Rape and plunder continued not far from her journey.

Any travelers would hear the baby's cries carried on the wind. Saren knelt over the ravaged infant, unable to soothe or comfort his pains of hunger.

The bread and rabbit dwindled. There was nothing to make broth with. To venture forth without Liam would only mean his death. Saren rocked back on her heels and did the only thing a desperate mother could do. She cradled the suffering babe and let him suckle her finger.

Hunger was his only disease, and his anguish and weakened body were his symptoms. Liam pulled and smacked Saren's finger with his mouth. The dawn faded while the baby suckled. Through the morning hours among the rocks, Saren's finger pacified the orphan to sleep.

Saren lay against a stone as she watched the infant sleep. She lay in the welcome silence with shut eyes, but no sleep would find her. She had to find food soon, or this solitude would be their doom.

Fog settled in the valley like a wet blanket. Though it protected her from being detected, Saren would not dare sleep.

Little Liam's breath was smooth and content for the first time. Saren smiled as she lay listening to his sleeping noises.

Rolling prone on the earth upon her woolen rags, Saren buried her tear- streaked face in her open hands. She was a strong girl, a proud and brave girl. Nevertheless, here, beyond anyone's gaze, she wept.

Her sobs had begun with gentle tears but consumed her body completely as the sun peeked into the summer sky. Somewhere before the day was gone, she found sleep because she was startled awake by the pound of thundering hooves. She rose and gathered her belongings in a single leap.

While remaining hidden, she held her breath. With a caress of her aching body, she stepped from her security of her hiding place, for she had no other alternative. She stepped into the uncertainty. Her hands pressed flat across her stomach; she moaned with hunger.

Wrapping her arms around herself to guard against the cool gust coming from between the once-sheltering rocks as she hummed Nan's ancient prayer,

"Hear, I beseech you, and be favorable to my prayer… and wisdom is justified of her sons." [6]

Saren ceased her song. She tried to listen to the night's noises, but all she could hear was the drumming of her heart in her chest.

As she listened for the approaching riders, Nan's prayer remained upon her lips, and she sang once more,

"… and wisdom is justified of her sons." [6]

Clarity swirled about her heart and through her mind as she gasped with knowing—a knowing with the certainty that is only carried by mothers across time. Saren knew the wisdom of love that her bound secret books contained and that the power that this wisdom processed threatened the Church's power. She knew the Church would stop at nothing to maintain control, and she was the only one alive to protect the sacred wisdom.

CHAPTER EIGHT

John Aston

Pottage warmed upon a scavenger's flame, shared from a carved platter, and a borrowed silver spoon was her blessing as Nan sought to locate her granddaughter and warn her of her pursuer.

The sun overhead warmed, but the warmth was only false, as the dank cold air penetrated each fiber it touched. "I thank ye kindly, sir, for feeding a traveling grandmamma so far from home."

"A grandmamma. I haven't had a grandma for years. Can you be my grandmamma, too?" he winked.

"Be your grandmamma?" She cupped her platter and sipped her broth. "I cannot be your grandmamma. I can be your friend." Wiping her sleeve across her brow, she asked, "And what might your name be?"

"John Aston of Oxford, my lady."

"I am pleased to make your acquaintance, Mr. Aston," Nan tasted her meal without revealing her starving appetite. "You may call me Nan. My name is Elle, but my family calls me Nan."

"I can't help but wonder, my lady, Nan, what brings you out and all alone to travel this dangerous road?"

Nan finished her humble meal. Wiping her mouth upon her apron, she spoke. "I'm searching for my granddaughter, Saren Eadwine. I must warn her of the trouble that seeks her." Hesitating, the old woman paused.

"Eadwine, you say?" John's question boomed. "I know your son, then, my lady." He smiled. "Yes. Charles and I have traveled in the same circles, sharing our message."

Nan's desperation grew, she continued. "Saren is quite small, though not as young as she appears." Nan smiled at the meekness and kindness of this man.

Mr. Aston listened while he finished the pottage after Nan had had her fill. Resuming her saga, she began this time at the beginning. "He was too accepting, too trusting of others, my son-in-law, Charles. Too trusting of his friends," she sighed. *Those he believed to be his friends*, she thought.

John offered to cook the old women more pottage. "My lady, I can refill the pot. I've plenty more," he assured her.

Smiling at his generosity, Nan thanked him and continued. "Charles's friend, his dear old friend Sir Percy, is now after my granddaughter. He knows she has what he's looking for;I I must find her and warn her."

"My lady, why do you worry so?"

"Because she has what he seeks, my friend. And they shall kill her to get it."

"It can't be as dangerous as that, can it, my lady?" asked Mr. Aston. "I fear so," she said. "I should be rid of this English Bible at my first opportunity."

"You are carrying an English Bible about the countryside, My Lady?" John's voice cracked higher than was natural. "That must also be what your granddaughter carries?"

Nan rose to remove her bundle from her shawl. "Would you like to have it? In payment for the warm meal? It shan't be of use to me," she explained. "I'm Pagan foremost, and I can't read a word even if I wanted."

"Yes, my lady." John reached for the worn book.

Nan sighed worriedly, "I couldn't leave it behind in Northumberland for that thief Lord Percy to take." She placed the Bible at John's feet. "Promise me that you will share it with those that can read, mind you?" The old woman wrapped her arms around her shoulders, hugging herself to warm her aged limbs and heart. "And just perhaps it will find its way to my Saren before I."

"Yes, perhaps," whispered John. "You say that your, Saren, girl is on her way to London?" he asked, holding the worn Bible. He pondered his words a moment and studied the book.

"Yes, John. Saren was instructed by her father to deliver the book she carries to Father Sautrey at Othy's Priory."

"Nan, My Lady. London is not the place for your granddaughter and her secret book, which I imagine to be unaccepted book of the New Testament." Looking into Nan's eyes, his scar across his cheekbone shining in the fire's glow, John Aston asked, "Dear lady. Will you travel with me? I will help you locate your granddaughter." John poked the fire to life with the blunt end of his spade. "The Church will stop at nothing to see those books destroyed. They ought to be taken at once to Dublin, then to the monks at Iona. Maybe farther." John set his meal aside and rose; strolling about the fire, he told Nan, "King Richard is now away to Ireland, participating in political advances there. Henry Bolingbroke, son of John

of Gaunt, Duke of Lancaster, and the third son of King Edward III met with the Archbishop of Canterbury and now enforce the De haecetico comburendo, allowing the burning of heretics, mainly to suppress the Lollard movement that threatened the church's authority over the people." John, kneeling facing Nan took her hand in his saying, "Your granddaughter will be killed… if she is found."

CHAPTER NINE

London's Gate

The horses were too many to count, all black against the fading light. Saren's hands trembled, not only from the chill. She caught the attention of one rider, perhaps the royal knights' leader.

Standing tall, her babe upon her hip, Saren faced him.

"Where are you going? Have you seen the raiders?" the rider barked. His mount trotted and pranced to the rhythm of Saren's heart.

"Yes, at the last village, but only one bandit remained behind the barn. However, that was days ago."

Tears on the cusp of falling from her timorous eyes, Saren spoke of fleeing the recent village.

"Aye, My Lady. The bandits are in protest of our new King Henry Bolingbroke," the rider told. "The raiders have presumably emerged from the north in search of treasure, though we've yet to apprehend them. Do you travel alone?" the knight asked.

Saren cast her gaze downward to the moss-covered rocks to conceal her, knowing that she, herself, was the treasure the raiders pursued.

The armor-clad rider circled his horse and motioned to another, then met him briefly in conversation drowned out by hooves clopping.

Saren, tempted to back away in fright, instead faced her fear to gain refuge.

Remaining tall in her stance, Saren wiped her skirt smooth, tamed her wild curls to the best of her ability, and sighed.

"We are breaking camp. Come south with us toward London unless you wish to be left here to fend for yourselves," the man suggested in a muffled whisper.

Tying her satchel upon her back, Saren used her cloak to swaddle Liam and secured him across her breast, freeing her arms. She hummed a ballad of her father's, a song he had played for her upon his pipes when they would sit and watch the sun rise or set over the water. Saren's motions became trance-like and effortless. The twilight air, heavy with the taste of the sea, rejuvenated her soul, giving her steps quickness as she walked forth.

Intent on her visitors, she did not notice the rider approaching from behind. His bark broke her trance. "Yeah, lady. You must come with me to London; no longer shall we, a battalion of soldiers, have your likes among us."

Saren turned to face this abrupt confrontation but immediately cast her gaze on her quiet infant, who tried to nuzzle at her breast.

She had little time to tighten the cloth that bound Liam and her possessions to her. The knight effortlessly swung Saren up behind him on his steed.

"Hold tight, My Lady. We ride to London." The horse exploded in thundering feet and flowing tail. Saren squeezed with every muscle in her legs and clung to the man before her with all her might.

She struggled to remain lost in her father's music of yesterday. She hummed the familiar tune of love to ensure her own bravery.

As Saren held on for her life and for the life of the child entrusted to her, she prayed. The even and smooth stride of the horse ensured the passage was bearable. The ground slipped by effortlessly beneath its prancing hooves. Saren rode behind the knight in gallant armor, her chin held high and eyes wide open. They rode undisturbed through the morning hours. All the while, neither her muscles nor her mind relaxed. At last, the crescent moon neared its height in the heavens, and the thundering hooves of the beast slowed to prance upon a ridge overlooking the city of London.

The closeness of the soldier's body to Saren was an entirely new sensation. As she steadied her child, quiet for the first moment in hours, her free arm closed around the massive body of the rider in front of her.

The cool air was filled with the scent of warm wool and un-soaped skin. Saren closed both eyes, remembering the smell of her father. The scent of another, this stranger near her, she breathed in with her eyes closed.

The clamoring of pounding hooves upon stone, the horse's rhythm, and the safety of a strong man all enabled Saren and her babe to tolerate their journey.

The discomfort became bearable through the distractions of her mind, and the journey was over just as it had begun.

Surrounded by a barricade and accessible only across the chain-braided gate, the city wall appeared all but unapproachable. Her mind on her destination, Saren had not prepared herself for the inevitable and abrupt dismount. Her wobbly legs reached the stone surface without warning and buckled on impact. Gathering her composure, Saren rose quickly to prevent herself and her child from being clipped by one of the flailing hooves.

The rider on the horse kept his voice close enough to be heard. "Say, 'Long live King Henry' at the gates below to be granted access, My Lady."

The mounted man did not wait for her reply or gratitude. Still, he pivoted his mount and galloped away without leaving his name or asking hers.

Hunger was her lone yearning, growing with each passing moment. The demand for food had ravished her spirit. She dreamed of venison and foods she had never tasted hours before the ride to London's city wall. And here, her knees trembled, her hands were clammy, and her cheeks flushed despite the cool breeze wafting upon her skin.

This new longing was bigger, fiercer than the hunger she had grown familiar with. She could not extinguish this hunger, and she closed her eyes as she watched the stranger ride beyond the ridge. Now, she must return to the demands of a somewhat lesser urgency, a hungry stomach.

Only the memory of his scent remained, which was no longer powerful enough to dissuade her empty stomach. Yet for those brief moments, the swift journey had delivered her beyond the pains of hunger to a place of longing that she had never been, the first stirrings of desire.

The sudden impact of the ground sent Liam into fits of rage from being so abruptly awoken from his dreams. Saren sat upon the rock to untie her passenger from his swaddling. The babe raged on in tears and screams, free to display his emotions. She cleaned him and then soothed him the best she could.

Saren and the child sat upon the cool stone, looking beyond the walls of London. The day encircled them with heavy clouds and warm rain.

Alone and now a surrogate mother, Saren marched forward to find refuge from the dangers of the solitude, humming her father's sweet melodies to a Pagan prayer of Nan's that rose to mingle about her like the stench of the waters of the Thames.

*"Lord and lady, twirl about, Guide me day and
night, throughout.*

*Guide me through each passing power. From head to
toe, from sky to ground,*

Keep us safe and well and sound,

*As those words I Pray to thee as I will it so
shall it be."[7]*

♦ ♦ ♦

A whisper of smoke lingered on the horizon, yet no commotion disturbed the crystalline aura. No percussions of battle drummed into the night as Saren approached the city's refuge.

Five rasps upon the fortress gate with the heavy knocker sent shivers along her spine.

If only the strong knight had delivered her within the walls. Then, she would be without hesitation.

Reciting the words "Hail King Henry," Saren's voice cracked before she had finished them and realized the king's name dared consume her. She was granted passage through the portal. A massive, barred iron gate rose just enough for her to duck beneath.

Clutching little Liam, her treasure, Saren arose to face the bewilderment of civilization, yes, and the dawning of a new king's arrival to claim the throne.

The stench of waste smacked Saren like a slap of a hand. She pinched her eyes and swallowed. Peering into her bundle, she lied, "We are safe here, my babe." She maneuvered forward, trusting her destination and her father's command.

Voices came from every crevice, some talking, some shouting—a cacophony of noise. Saren wandered among the people, the horses, and the filth to find the night's lodging.

A great stone barn and stable welcomed her near the river's edge. Two tall doors remained ajar to the rear of the structure for the refugees to enter, and Saren tucked unnoticed into the building. No food would be found that night. Finding an empty stall with loose bedding strung about, she claimed a quiet, dark corner. She fashioned a bed for herself and babe as she thought *tomorrow's dawn would bring our salvation.* Not daring to light a candle to read from her notes, Saren remembered more of Joseph's reading aboard the Al-Aoura: *"What is the sin of the world?" Then she remembered his last reading, which stopped midsentence: "He does not see through the soul nor through the spirit, but the mind that is between the two that is what sees the vision, and it is…"* Saren slept.

The light had yet to penetrate the stable as Saren gathered her camp and left the safety of its walls to reveal the city center where carts stood selling cloth, scented soaps, and treats.

Saren strolled among the carts, looking for something to eat and looking for the merchant, Jon the mute, whom her father had sent her to find.

The street was peaceful, though lifeless, and dimly lit. Saren walked among the merchants' carts with purpose, disguising her fears, though desperation hung noticeable around her. Approaching a younger merchant setting up to sell knives and blades of various lengths, she inquired about any employment he might provide her. His shunning was like a rebuke given to a dog. Saren pressed on. *My hopelessness cloaks me like Liam's hungry cry,* she thought.

Though kinder in their rejections, the following early vendors she approached were less than enthused about her request.

The last cart on the street stood erect upon blocks of wood. No wheels remained beneath, for there it must have sat, a fixture of the central square, always. A wary man sat near, watching the citizens' comings and goings. Saren stopped and spoke, "Good day, sir." She nodded a subtle curtsy. "May I find sustenance here, sir, for my babe and I?" she asked hopefully. Looking up at the ancient eyes hovering, she had but a sweet smile to give in exchange for bread. Her stomach began to hearken in hunger since her last meal was robbed from a rebel's camp.

His smile revealed only two, or maybe three, teeth. Nonetheless, his expression was kind, yet surprised by Saren's acknowledgment. All alone, the old merchant must not have received many kind words. Surrounded by life, untouched by it, nor a participant in it, the old man seemed delighted in Saren's company.

He smiled without any acknowledgment of her request. Again, she repeated her question, and he only smiled in return.

"Humph," Saren grumbled. "Can you hear what I speak?" she asked the little man. Again, he only smiled in response as the sun teased forth to a musky dawn.

At last, he touched her arm, raised his hand to his ear, and pointed skyward. Saren looked blankly at him, and then she heard it, too. The music of pipes from far off touched her ears. The song she knew and hummed along. The little man clapped and danced to his own melody.

Pursing her lips, she opened her bundle to reveal her urgency for help: the baby, wide-eyed yet quiet.

Once glorious with youth, his indigo eyes peered over Saren's shoulder while his feet still danced upon the dirt.

He reached into the baby's bundle and touched her book beneath. Saren returned his friendly smile and touched her fingertips to her lips, then to the babe's, saying, "Hungry."

Realization swarmed across his pruned face, taking with it all trace of his smile. Without a response, he turned and scurried away, leaving Saren alone with his merchandise of tools and hardware. Discouraged, she remained determined to fulfill her father's request to deliver the secret book and waited.

CHAPTER TEN

Bosworth

How can I warn the innocent of Bolingbroke's arrival?" Charles asked the heavens. "There is still time."

He leaped down, keeping his pipes and his spirit ever flowing. Walking on and looking back once to count his followers, he marched toward the setting sun.

Charles reached the city perimeter that would serve as their cover. Men and boys scurried for weapons and shields for battle. Families remained; fathers, brothers, and sons united. A barricade was being built along the shoulder of the village. There, men could take cover or house their ambush.

Walking among the people, Charles offered encouraging words to each. No man heard his voice, only he. At last, Charles chose an angelic station among the lads. Hiding along the barricade, he played.

Charles played for King Richard's entourage as they hurried northward, a ballad of urgency, the music of war.

The men and boys of Bosworth could only wait and watch Bolingbroke's men approaching as they built up massive fires and prepared.

Their fears would have been satisfied if Bolingbroke's men attempted aggression before dusk. They sat nearby waiting, listening, and watching with trepidation as all hope of defense was threatened.

Charles played the separate drones at wide intervals, hoping to keep the soldiers focused. The magnitude of warriors from the camps overpowered all the chanter Charles could muster, washing away his rhythm with the moonlight. On he played through the night's end and against the winds.

No one slept on the barricade. Charles's music played on while sunlight made its way down the hillside. Charles intended to stay there with the young men beside him on the front, the young men who asked throughout the night if they were going to die. And oft, those same boys would ask, looking through Charles's soul without seeing him, "Does anyone else hear the piping?"

A smile filled Charles's heart as he filled the bellows and played a heavenly serenade.

The young man cried then, the tears for a lifetime not yet complete. Someone nearby yelled, "King Richard's traitors are moving nearer now. Be ready!" Henry Bolingbroke's men encroached upon the tired battalion.

Charles had no weapon for battle. All he held to his body were his bone pipes, and he played the song of battle again.

The conspirators arrived in haste; silently, they neared. Charles played loud, from higher ground, into the day's fate. His chanter echoed to strengthen his fellow men from the impending battle. The lad beside Charles crouched on the barricade with a sword poised in hand. He awaited his potential doom. Men arrived in swarms. The lad retained his stance. Charles played on, not knowing this soldier's name. He played a bravery march for him.

The soldiers met the villagers' resistance. The lad held on to his defense with every octave that Charles held. Men and boys along the wall fled to save themselves. The men-at-arms closer to Charles listened to his melody, consciously or unconsciously.

Charles's music resonated through the fighting. The remaining sailors and men were spent, beaten, bruised, and weather-laden. They surrendered their King Richard without a sufficient fight. The submissive King Richard's men realized too late their betrayal and relented. One thing remained: the necessity to fight: love for home, heritage, and brothers. This was every warrior's worn face. Charles played with the intensity provided by the heavens. He strolled the road with his pipe crescendo, serenading in the hope that peace would one day prevail.

The daylight hours fled, and with it, the evidence of victory. Fires smoldered among the ruins, and the living laid the unfortunate dead to rest.

The celebration of the fall of a king ensued as though a battle had erupted above the horizon. The splendor of the display grew frightening as he neared. Never had Charles witnessed such a display of untold power. Hesitating below the revelry, he observed the insanity of it all.

With a shake of his hairy head and a blink of his eyes, he neared the mass of people. Knowing the opposing presence was that of the new King Henry Bolingbroke, Charles kept his presence toward the inland realm and his fellow men-at-arms and their grievances'.

The armsmen lay prone on the rocks while their horses pranced in nervous excitement. However, though the king's men outnumbered their oppressors, the chatter of despair and harried plans of surrender rose among them. Onward, Charles traveled until compelled to rest among the besieged.

Kneeling there, surrounded by fear and uncertainty, Charles watched for anyone to establish a defensive maneuver on King Richard's behalf. Knights and men-at-arms, all fellow English countrymen, crouched on the ground with faces covered with rags. Fear and pride left back upon the shores of Wales; King Richard's regiment folded. A man half Charles's age sprang to his feet and fled. The remaining countrymen gathered for support, questioning their fate.

Charles played. He played for the soldiers who remained and for those who fled in haste, for the weak, the lonely. Charles played for King Richard.

◆　　　◆　　　◆

The casualties were counted, identified, and removed. Victorious, Henry Bolingbroke's cost was small.

Charles walked among the wounded, playing a song of hope and life to free their souls like a prayer. His irrelevant mission to share the English Bibles ceased, and now his only mission was to help his daughter. Charles would refuse heaven if given the opportunity. He carried a personal duty to see his daughter, his Saren, to safety. Charles continued his struggle toward redemption, another battle, or another war to prove his bravery. Charles, no longer in this earthly realm, had proven his bravery, yet he remained. Helping Saren, then, must be his only means of gaining heaven.

He walked on into the night, leaving the sound of death behind. Charles's steps were slow and deliberate, and the weight of sorrow hung in the fog before him. This battle was lost, but bravely, he confronted fear with his song. Song was all he possessed and would be all he could give.

His passage of time in this dimension, between heaven and earth, was no longer linear but as transparent as the sea's surface. His eyes had not closed while the moon waned, then waxed again. On Charles sang his love through the bone pipes; neither urgency nor passion woke him from this trance as he played. Fueled by heavenly energy, the positive light of love is neither a dreary shiver nor a cry.

Like a rainbow's caress or a cool breeze rustling the trees on a hot day, the energy of such departed souls meanders, lingering behind with the living to fulfill one step toward paradise. Finishing their unfinished work, saying goodbye to loved ones, or something more specific, like staying back to protect a child.

CHAPTER ELEVEN

Jon the Mute

The fragile man with indigo eyes soon returned, watching the faces of passersby. He clutched a small satchel tightly to his breast and carried a worn leather broth pouch. He licked his lips repeatedly.

Spotting him among the bustle, Saren returned to him. His eyes still a- twinkle, the depth of the blue endless, he thrust the small parcel at Saren without one spoken word. He then handed her the liquid-filled pouch and pointed away, returning to his trove of merchandise.

Saren looked toward the direction of his gesture, but nothing awaited there.

Instead, she followed behind, if for nothing more than to thank the kind man for his offering.

As Saren approached the wagon of metal goods, the gracious man sitting beneath the soiled leather canopy refused to look into her face. Reaching out with her trembling hand, she was aghast at the filth caked there beneath her own fingernails and upon her flesh. She pulled her hand back as if a flame had licked her skin.

Folding her hands under the baby and her newly acquired satchel of goods, she spoke, sure the mute man could not hear, "Thank ye, my kind soul," knowing this was Jon the Mute that her father sent her to seek.

Gazing up at her, the twinkle had returned to his eye, and he gave a quick shake of his head, then looked away.

Saren stole away to find an overturned barrel beside the stone wall of the fortress. Shaded from the late morning sun, she unswaddled the bundled babe. His skin, though warm, was ashen and pale. Neither fits nor tears stirred the babe's blood. Yet this quiet filled Saren with fear of his death. She had seen this many times upon the little faces that her mother had borne years past. Babes given sparingly and taken too quickly. The siblings she had hoped for, the boys her parents longed for, prepared for, and created, were all lost in the night, too fragile to remain.

With each infant's death, Saren had lost part of herself, gone eternally.

She rubbed Liam's skin with her palms, gentle circles at first. The tears fell behind her lashes. She rubbed the small body, then swaddled him again and put the leather bong of broth to his lips. He suckled dry one moment before returning to unconsciousness. She tried waking him, though futilely.

Opening her small satchel, a gift from the blue-eyed man, she touched the contents.

The package was firm yet pliable, and it did not feel edible. Saren opened the packet just a bit further to reveal a manuscript drawn with ink on bound papers. The writing was legible if only she were literate in the Hebrew lettering on them.

Her eyes wide, Saren touched the tip of her tongue to the roof of her mouth. She refolded the leather flaps and rewound the strap that bound the bundled books. Thinking it snug beneath her weak babe, she rose to locate the Mute and return his unopened parcel, not noticing the loaf of brittle bread wrapped beneath.

The crowds along the cobblestone street pushed past. Saren had not ambled far from the rickety wooden treasure cart, but soldiers lined the street as she returned.

The mute slip of a man she had unknowingly accepted the bundled package from was held between two leather-armored brutes. He kicked and shrieked, his mouth smeared with blood, as he demanded release, though his words were inaudible. His eyes ablaze with fear told all.

He spotted Saren there among the onlookers. The sight of her must have calmed him. For one heartbeat, their eyes locked. Without blinking, his fight subsided. He mouthed what Saren recognized as "Stay back."

One soldier pulled him while shouting in his ear. The man wearing the new Crown's colors leaned toward him as the blue-eyed man pointed his bound wrists west across the crowded street, away from where Saren stood.

Saren watched the seized man with averted eyes. Whatever she now possessed was not meant to be in her hands. Reflex, coupled with her flight response and the power to flee, was Saren's best defense. She ran.

The mass of people propelled her into a narrow alley where a trumpet sounded, babies cried, and people shouted.

The corridor opened to a grand display of stone steps and pillars encircled in each direction by stone stairs to serve as seating places for an audience.

Voices shrieked among the onlookers as the men-at-arms pushed through the masses of people. Saren struggled to see what was happening, but keeping her footing required her utmost concentration.

The crowds stopped pushing, and she could finally clamber atop a higher step to witness the occasion.

A lone horseman entered through the narrow street. Saren watched, hopeful to recognize the man who had kindly escorted her last night and awakened such an unfamiliar longing of her flesh; she cast her face downward to hide her rosy color.

The armored soldiers looked alike except for the crest upon her escort's breastplate. The mounted knights stood at the center on adorned horses, facing the one approaching. Many more soldiers armed in leathers marched two-by-two along the way to stand at attention before the horsemen. The remaining escorted the seized man with indigo eyes to take him to the city center.

The hamlet center, where a raised scaffold was built around a single pole, and rocks from the Thames were stacked beneath the pole to support it above the crowd's view. There, the mute man was tied. His back against an iron pole, they secured his head upright with a leather strap. Books and rubbish were piled at his feet. The people shouted and cheered. Villagers lit the papers among the stones and ignited the piled fuel.

Saren covered her mouth with her hand to silence her protest. Remembering Joseph's words upon the Al-Aoura, *The Savior said,'Do not lay down any rules beyond what I appointed you, and do not give a law like the lawgiver lest you be constrained by it.'*

Saren's dry screams tore from her throat. Witnesses to this execution turned to her. Their eyes fell upon her from afar, yet the frail, bound man turned his eyes to the flames below without protesting.

Overcoming her shock, Saren stood frozen among the spectators.

"This man is found guilty of heresy!" the one higher-ranked knight from horseback declared. His horse pranced and then stomped upon the hard-packed earth. "He has been sentenced to public execution in accordance with the 'De heretico comburendo' law regarding the burning of heretics." A roar erupted from the spectators.

The man tried to lift his head to the sounds that he could feel around him. No emotion showed on his face, only the placid look of a man before his unjust execution. Then he spotted Saren through the smoke, standing among the people. His stare was frozen like ancient ice. Saren ceased to breathe.

Weak cries of hunger escaped her swaddled robe. Saren dropped his gaze of ice. The man, however, kept his eyes upon her as she tended her child. She moved uneasily under the blueness of his watch as it penetrated her aura.

"Ruith!" came a Gaelic cry of the old man. Saren dared not glance up or run but kept her needed attention on her infant starving in her arms.

The man, presumed mute, had spoken, but Saren dared not make eye contact again as she glanced toward him. His eyes penetrated her being, and his next word sent a chill across the wind. "Run!" he managed to cry, this time in English, through long-unused lips.

Whatever her satchel contained, Saren would not eat that day. He spoke no more. As he was gagged and the fires fueled higher, Saren dared glance only once to see all eyes from the army were primed, waiting for one to flee. She stepped ever so nimbly to the crowd's edge to find a place to attempt to pacify her babe. No eyes suspected her as an accomplice. *An accomplice to the heresy of The Crown*, she imagined.

◆　◆　◆

Liam suckled from the leather pouch, taking weak tastes of salty broth. His reflex to nurse had grown weaker.

Saren had swaddled and held too many lifeless babes for her mother. She had a fierce determination to rear this child as her own flesh. Her sorrowful heart poured forth with love for him as she had for all her mother's departed babes. She silently prayed to find a way to exchange her acquired goods for nourishment.

The mute man's shaky words had shattered the silence across the square above the mass of voices. He had directed the words to Saren in kindness.

However, evil witnessed her rapid departure, as evidenced by the many onlooking warriors who scanned the crowd for anyone who would dare flee.

The infant's croons had ceased. No longer did her tiny bundle call for sustenance. This lack of crying, this quiet, startled Saren back from her fearful trance. She lowered her gaze from the execution, thus breaking any association with the mute.

Saren stood waiting among the city walls, her head hanging down to avoid the authorities' eyes. She stood, avoiding the old mute's recognition once more. He would not speak out of her identity, even if it would save his own life.

The guards struggled to follow the old man's eyes through the growing smoke.

Though the blue eyes followed her still, he did not shout again. So there Saren stood with head hung low, rocking to and fro, her starving babe wrapped in swaddling cloth at her breast, as she listened to the snapping and popping as the flames consumed the books piled at the mute's feet.

The moment of flight had come for Saren as she held her motionless infant close. She silently fled. She pushed through the shouting masses to the center's edge. An open street lay in her path, but someone grabbed her before she could gain the cover of a door.

A cold, wet hand closed around her wrist from behind. The firm grasp jerked her around and away from freedom. An elderly, frail woman stood before her. "You, you are running away, girl." A chuckle raged through her hideous body. "Here, I have a girl," the woman hollered toward the crowded street.

Saren jerked and pulled, unable to escape the malicious woman's clasp. Though she appeared tiny and frail, she was strong and determined.

Saren's hungry body struggled. The old and fragile woman was more muscular and better fed than Saren. The stranger held fast to her free arm.

"Here, I have the girl. Here, guards." The old woman's voice trembled with excitement.

The quiver of the woman's voice filled Saren's ears, sending anger through her veins. She looked at the woman's face, only to be met with eyes filled with pain—a pain from a soul abused and forgotten.

Saren looked into the abyssal eyes. The hollowness there shone through her, shattering her restraint. The desire to be free of the woman's evil clutch fueled her strength.

The old woman's calls had brought eyes upon them. Saren glanced beyond the woman's shoulder to see guards looking in their direction. One man mouthed words and rocked his arms, cradling an imaginary infant. Their eyes seized Saren's. Fearful to break the cold stare, Saren subtly shook her head and shouted, "No."

The guard shoved past the crowd, leaped from the raised platform, and pushed through in Saren's direction.

CHAPTER TWELVE

A New King

The country had been ransacked; blood was spilled upon the kingdom's flag. Charles's soul's presence now had a purpose and a heavenly reason to linger, to wander. Charles left the church searching for people his music might save and other souls he could inspire to heaven.

Charles walked the beaches. His pipes hung across his shoulders, clicking together as he stepped. The waves lapped gently, licking the rocks along the coast. The moonlight that remained graced the last stars of the morning sky.

Charles traveled toward civilization, toward people, toward the dawning of a new king's reign.

With a poisoned laugh full of venomous saliva, the old woman clasped Saren now with both arms.

Because Saren dared not release her clutch on the ever-still infant, she had no choice but to lunge backward. She pulled the evil woman who held her in bondage close to her body. The old woman's haggard eyes widened in disbelief as she was pulled forward against her will. Saren thrust her knee with an unconscious strength into the woman's belly.

Air escaped her with a surge. The old hag loosened her hold as she doubled over with the unexpected impact.

Saren instinctively thought she would flee from the evil snare, but before she ran, she looked down at the nasty old woman and offered her hand to help her stand. The hag refused. Saren dared not look at any of the many passersby as she exhaled a long-held breath. She turned to the street and the direction she had been shoved. She returned to the market square lined with carts and goods for sale, the only place where she could find sustenance for herself and her babe.

Sea air brought inland with the Thames, lingered among the constant voices of endless chatter in London's city center. A silence descended over the crowd once the flames burnt out. Saren's head jerked up to the lull. The remains of her mute acquaintance dangled from the blackened post. Saren closed her eyes before him and whispered her grandmamma's Pagan prayer:

*"Lord and Lady grant me the power of water, to
accept what I cannot change The power of Fire, for
energy and courage to change the things
that I can The Power of Air, for the ability
to know the difference*

*Grant me the Power of Earth, for the strength to
know and walk my path."*[8]

The afternoon sun penetrated the encroaching mist. It warmed her slightly and began drying her skin and clothes.

She hurried lightly across the cobbled street avoiding the eyes of passersby and desperate not to attract attention to herself. A young lad, about the same age as she, took her by the elbow.

His rough hand, larger than Saren's, held to her arm like a guardian, and she followed in desperation. Too exhausted to protest, he led her through the streets. Saren's options were spent. She had no family to call upon, no money, no lodging, no food, and the one she was seeking and found had been arrested and burned alive at the stake.

The only certainty of this day for Saren was the sun sinking lower in the vacant sky—and the growl of her empty stomach.

Any crumb of sustenance that she had found she had chewed, softened, and then given to Liam. His crying now ceased. He was either sleeping contently, rocked by Saren's rapid movements, or dead. She did not look.

The satchel she lugged now grew heavy. As Saren struggled to keep up with the young lad's pace, he led her on.

Turning from the direction of their haste, but only a moment, Saren imagined the mob in pursuit. She hurried with her newfound accomplice.

They hurried between buildings, ducking down corridors and through crowded streets of people and horses. Saren did not know where he was taking her or who he was but facing the cries of the angry people was not an option.

Jon, the mute, had been arrested. Whatever the contents of her satchel that Saren now carried slung across her back, the mob and the guards were after. On she ran, following the boy.

He led her up a flight of rickety stairs and through a narrow door. There they stopped and watched as the street below filled with the growing mass of people, then cleared. Their breathing slowed, but neither of their hearts quit racing. The boy turned to look at Saren, and a shy grin shone from the natural twinkle in his eyes.

"Good day, My Lady," he spoke as his eyes blinked in the dimmed light and the sweat ran across his brow. "The ugly old woman whom you helped off the street pointed you out. Don't you know?" Soiled yellow curls fell out from beneath a battered cap. "My name is William Wynch, but you may call me Will." The lad attempted a true smile, and his bare feet were restless upon the old wood.

"Thank you for your troubles." Saren reluctantly dropped his hand. "My name is Saren, Saren Eadwine."

My Lady, Saren." His feet ceased their shuffle upon the dusty floor. "Come, for we shall fetch my ma." William took Saren's hand once more in his own. "She may know what we are to do. That was my pa's friend Jon who was arrested, you see?" His eyes grew wider as he explained, "Yeah, I'd just ventured in to ask him if he'd heard news of my pa's whereabouts. Come." William led Saren deeper into the poorly lit clapboard building that was built from a skeleton of beams and joined with the support of stones piled at the corners.

Not until they reached the lower floor and an open window to the street did Saren dare peek in on Liam.

His tiny eyes, though open as if witnessing the chase, were ashen and sunken. Saren moistened her thumb in her own mouth before trying to offer it to her little passenger to suckle. The familiar look of death upon the babe's face began to slowly chisel into Saren's reality.

"He's a hungry boy," William whispered glancing down into Saren's arms. "How old is your babe?"

Saren looked up, startled by the notion of Liam being her own babe, but only grinned and gave a shrug of her tired shoulders. "No teeth yet, so I'd guess that he must be no more than eight months." Saren closed her eyes for an instant in thought and said, "And yes, he is quite hungry. We both are." This comment made her mouth water.

"You aren't sure how old your babe is, then?" William's brow creased between his eyes.

"No, silly." Saren patted his shoulder. "He is not really my babe. I am just a girl, you see. I found him… I rescued him while on my journey here. His mother, I found dead in a raided village. She was clutching him beneath her. Nearly squished, he was, the poor-wee lad."

"Ugh, then." William's smile once more disappeared. "Why was his mother dead?" The lad's eyes widened. "Was it Bolingbroke's men? I would guess so, indeed," he continued. "We'd best hurry on before the mob returns."

Keeping her thoughts to herself, Saren did not mention *Percy's mob searching for her.*

They continued across the way. William led her through a rusted iron gate. "You say you know the man who was arrested today, Will?"

"Yes, I do."

"Why did those guards take him away?"

"His name is Jon." Taking a heavy breath, Will explained, "I don't know why he was arrested. And I don't know why my father has disappeared." Reaching a weathered door, William turned the tarnished knob and entered a cozy room. A small fire blazed and hissed in the home's fireplace. "I heard someone call the mute a 'Lollard'. I also watched him watching you, Saren, like the old nasty woman who grabbed you." Will grew teary and looked to his bare feet. "My pa's been arrested for heresy. Lollards are being arrested and burned at the stake for heresy like Jon the Mute. No trial or jury is called." Will glanced up as his tears fell to the hard-packed earthen floor.

A small, frail woman scurried into the room, her feet shuffling upon the dirt floor as she hurried. "William, Will, my boy. Where have you been? I was worried, child." Her large eyes, twinkling despite the poorly lit room, shone just as William's. She looked to Saren, who shifted under the weight of her load.

"What have you brought home today, my son?" Her smile was also as persistent as her son's.

Saren's body went limp as she slowly approached the small woman, passing her tender package off and dropping to the ground in exhaustion.

A note from the author

I invite you to join our voices in conversation and in a song about the Morningstar series: Saren's journey of divination as a body and soul in Man's world, listening to the voice of love within. The God within.

Please join Morningstar's group here to learn of upcoming books in the series:

https://www.facebook.com/groups/booksforgirls

About The Author

Ondi Laure is a fifth-generation native of Wyoming, renowned for her novels that delve into humanity's untamed past. In her acclaimed book, *Morningstar*, she explores untold histories, wisdom, and the courage of those who defended the repressed sacred truths of the universe. For over ten years, Ondi has guided others in aligning with their story's purpose and embracing their identity as authors. Her expertise has been recognized by *Forbes* and *Top Talent* magazines.

To learn more about the author, Book Three and her Aligned Writing Program visit: https://MyInkLinks.com

Cited Sources

1,7 Bible Manuscript Society, 1382 Wycliffe Bible; https://biblemanuscriptsociety.com/Bible-resources/ English-Bible-History/Wycliffe-Bible

Coogan, M. A Brief Introduction to the Old Testament: The Hebrew Bible in its Context. (Oxford University Press: Oxford 2009). p. 369; (Psalm 78:14)

https://greywolf.druidry.co.uk/2013/04/12th-century-english-prayer-tomother- earth

2,8 Grey Wolf. A Prayer to Mother Earth: 12th Century. https://greywolf.druidry.co.uk/2013/04/12th-century-english- prayer-to-mother-earth/

Luminarium. Anthology of English Literature, "The Ballad of Chevy Chase." http://www.luminarium.org/medlit/ medlyric/chevychase.htm

Pagels, "What Became of God the Mother?" in Womanspirit Rising. Carol P. Christ and Judith Plaskow (Harper & Row, 1979), 109.

Parrott, Douglas M. The Sophia of Jesus Christ: 2001-2020. http://www.earlychristianwritings.com/text/sophia.html

Stephan Patterson & Marvin Meyer. The Gnostic Society Library, The Nag Hammadi Library. The Gospel of Thomas. http://gnosis.org/naghamm/gosthom.html

Textus Receptus. John Wycliffe Bible 1382, Proverbs 8:22-23, 27,30. http://textusreceptusbibles.com/

Wycliffe Associates and Simons, Keith. Easy English Bibles: 2005. https://www.easyenglish.bible/ The Sophia of Jesus Christ hppt://www.earlychirstianwritings.com/text/Sophia.html

www.ingramcontent.com/pod-product-compliance
Lightning Source LLC
Chambersburg PA
CBHW071945190726
48293CB00004B/1364